The Marmalade Pony

"There's a surprise for you at home," said Dad.

"What is it?"

Dad wouldn't say. He made Hannah wait all the way home. What could it be? she thought. One of her friends from her old school, coming to tea? His new wardrobe? For a wild, ridiculous moment she thought it might be a pony. Perhaps he'd brought Marmalade home . . .

LINDA NEWBERY

The Marmalade Pony

Illustrated by Susan Hellard

To Mariam

Scholastic Children's Books,
Scholastic Publications Ltd,
7–9 Pratt Street, London NW1 0AE, UK

Scholastic Inc.,
555 Broadway, New York, NY 10012-3999, USA

Scholastic Canada Ltd,
123 Newkirk Road, Richmond Hill,
Ontario, Canada L4C 3G5

Ashton Scholastic Pty Ltd,
P O Box 579, Gosford, New South Wales,
Australia

Ashton Scholastic Ltd,
Private Bag 92801, Penrose, Auckland,
New Zealand

First published in the UK by Scholastic Publications Ltd, 1994

Text copyright © Linda Newbery, 1994
Illustrations copyright © Susan Hellard, 1994

ISBN 0 590 55742 4

Typeset by Contour Typesetters, Southall, London
Printed by Cox & Wyman Ltd, Reading, Berks.

10 9 8 7 6 5 4 3 2 1

Chapter 1

Hannah didn't think she was going to like the new house. It was small, with a little wedge of scrappy garden. All the rooms needed decorating and the bathroom had damp marks on the walls. The road outside was so busy that she wasn't allowed to cross it by herself.

She would have to go to a new school. She felt lonely and missed her friends. There seemed to be no children in their new road. Most of the neighbours were much older than Mum and Dad, with children who had grown up and gone to live somewhere else.

The only person of Hannah's age was a dark-haired girl who sometimes played in the garden next door. Dad said she must be the granddaughter of the man who

lived there. She didn't live there – she only came on Saturdays.

There was no one for Hannah to be friends with.

"You'll make new friends at school," Mum said. "It won't seem so bad in a week or two."

Mum had left her friends behind, too. She was trying very hard to be cheerful. So was Dad. Sometimes you could *hear* them trying to be cheerful, both at once.

"We're lucky I've got my part-time job," Mum said. "Some families are worse off."

Dad just grunted and turned the page of the newspaper. Every Friday, he got up early and went to the newsagent's along the road to buy the local paper. Then he sat down busily at the table with a cup of coffee and a red pen, reading every single job advertisement. By Friday evening, after making lots of phone calls and visits to the Job Centre, he was fed up again. There were so many people looking for jobs.

There was only one good thing about the new house as far as Hannah could see. It was nearer to the country than their old house had been, and there was a riding school along the lane. There were stables and barns, and several ponies grazed in a field where jumps were set up. There were ponies of all colours – black, brown, chestnut, white, and a spotty one like a Dalmatian dog. At weekends, and sometimes in the evenings, processions of riders made their way past the house, on their way to the woods. Hannah looked enviously out of the window. Some of the riders were about her age.

"Oh, Dad," she burst out. "Could I...?"

She stopped, seeing Dad's face. No, of course she couldn't. It would cost too much. But Dad said they'd go down and see. Hannah already wished she hadn't asked, especially when they got to the riding school gate and read the board outside. Lessons £7 per hour, it said. Dad had had to sell the car when he lost his job

at the steelworks, because a car cost too much to keep. Of course he couldn't afford £7 for riding lessons. Just once, perhaps, for a birthday present, but not every week. To learn to ride properly you had to go every week.

Dad looked just as disappointed as Hannah.

"I'm sorry, love," he said, as they turned away. "If only it wasn't such an *expensive* hobby."

"It doesn't matter," Hannah said.

They walked along beside the field with the red-and-white poles and barrels in it. Some of the ponies were grazing there, and one of them came up to the fence. It was a small pony, the one Hannah liked best. She had watched them go past the window so often that she knew them all.

This one was the colour of caramel, or sticky toffee, or marmalade – the dark kind with thick slices of peel in it. The marmalade pony was usually at the back, jogging along on quick little hooves to keep up with the bigger ponies. It had a bushy mane and forelock the colour of straw, and bright, mischievous eyes. It came up to Hannah and pushed at her hand with its soft nose, as if it knew her.

"This is my favourite," Hannah said.

"I wonder what his name is?" Dad said.

Hannah thought for a minute. "I don't think he's a he," she said. "I think she's a she, and her name ought to be Marmalade."

Dad laughed. "*Marmalade!* I've heard of a marmalade cat, but not a marmalade pony."

"This is one," Hannah said, and she picked some grass for Marmalade, even though there was plenty of grass in the field for the ponies to eat. Marmalade ate it, and Hannah pretended for a moment or two that Marmalade was her own pony. There was nothing to stop her pretending. You don't need money to pretend.

Chapter 2

Dad started behaving very oddly. As well as doing the shopping and cooking, and hunting for a job, he started doing something in the little garden shed. No one was allowed to go in. Once Hannah heard sawing and banging and wondered what he was making. A boat, perhaps? He liked boats. But the sea was miles and miles away.

Perhaps Dad was pretending, too.

Next Saturday morning she found a long list on the kitchen table, in Dad's writing. It said:

Primer
Wool
glue
Varnish.
leather
Pole
Felt
Curtain rings

Just as Hannah was picturing a glued-together varnished boat, with billowing leather sails tied on with woollen ropes, Dad shouted, "Don't look at that! It's a —"

He snatched the list from her.

"A what?" Hannah said.

"A – a shopping list. Just some things for the house," Dad said, walking quickly out of the kitchen.

Hannah went into the garden, where Mum was planting tulip bulbs so that the garden would have some colour in it next spring.

"What's Dad making in the shed?" Hannah asked.

"Oh – a something. A – a wardrobe," Mum said. "Yes, a wardrobe. That's what he said it was."

Hannah felt disappointed. The boat with leather sails would have been more

interesting. All the same, she thought, it must be a very *unusual* wardrobe to need all those ingredients.

For the next few evenings, Dad stayed out of the shed, although Hannah noticed that he smelled of paint. On Wednesday afternoon, he met Hannah at the school gates, looking pleased and excited.

"Have you got a job?" Hannah cried.

"No," Dad said. "But there's a surprise for you at home."

"What is it?"

Dad wouldn't say. He made Hannah wait all the way home. What could it be? she thought. One of her friends from her old school, coming to tea? His new wardrobe? For a wild, ridiculous moment she thought it might be a pony. Perhaps he'd brought Marmalade home . . .

Dad took her into the living room and made her sit down.

"Now shut your eyes and wait for a minute."

Hannah closed her eyes and listened hard. She almost expected to hear the clop of polished hooves on the floor. But there was no sound, and then Dad said eagerly, "You can open them now."

Hannah looked. There was Dad, holding a stick with a wooden pony's head. It was varnished in a colour like toffee or caramel or marmalade, and it had a bushy mane like Marmalade's, made of thick cream-coloured wool. It had little curved ears made of felt. It had painted nostrils and a mouth, and round eyes like buttons. It even had a bridle made from strips of green leather, with big curtain rings for the bit.

"What do you think?" Dad said, full of pride.

"Isn't it lovely?" said Mum, who had followed him in.

Hannah stared. It was only a toy pony –
a hobby-horse. How silly she had been to
think it might have been a real one! But
Mum and Dad were so delighted with it
that she said, "Thanks, Dad. It's great."
And she stroked its mane and pretended
to ride it, holding the green reins and
galloping three times round the garden.
Dad fetched his camera and took some
photos.

"What will you call him?" Mum said.

Hannah thought for a moment. "I
don't think he's a he," she said. "I think
she's a she, and her name's Marmalade."

Dad puffed out his breath with relief. "I
hoped you'd say that."

"Why?" said Hannah.

"Come and see," shouted Dad, and he
raced up the stairs, followed by Hannah,
Marmalade and Mum.

Hannah stopped in her bedroom door-
way and stared. "It's a stable for
Marmalade!"

"That's right," Dad said, proudly. "Be
careful. The paint's not dry."

Dad had cut Hannah's wardrobe door
in half so that the top part swung open,
like a real stable. Over the top, he had
fixed a green plaque, with MARMALADE
painted on it in marmalade-coloured
letters.

23

Hannah put Marmalade into her stable. She looked so funny with her head poking out from all the T-shirts and jeans that Hannah laughed.

"I'll be able to lie in bed and look at my own pony in her stable," she said.

Dad looked so pleased that Hannah wished he had a horse and stable of his own.

Chapter 3

That night, Hannah looked at Marmalade for a long time before she went to sleep. Marmalade was only a toy, but in the semi-darkness Hannah could pretend she was real. The street light outside threw Marmalade's shadow against the wall, outlining her pricked ears and tufty mane.

Hannah slept, and then something woke her up, something that sounded like a hoof stamping impatiently. She opened her eyes and looked towards the stable door. She thought she saw Marmalade toss her head, throwing back her thick mane.

"Come on, then," Marmalade said. "What are you waiting for?"

Hannah sat straight up in bed. "You can talk!"

Marmalade snorted. "Yes, of course."

"But you're only a . . ."

"Only a what?" Marmalade said, with a trace of annoyance.

"Only a – well, a toy."

"Hrrrmmpphhh!" Marmalade said, in

the sneezy way ponies have. "In the daytime, perhaps. Night-time is different. Now, are you coming or not?"

"But where are we going?"

"For a ride, of course. Now, if you'd kindly unbolt my stable door . . ."

Hannah got out of bed and slid back the bolt on Marmalade's door. Funny – she didn't remember noticing a bolt there before.

"Thank you," Marmalade said politely as the door swung open. She clopped out of the stable, four shiny hooves on

cobblestones. She arched her neck proud-
ly and jingled the bit in her mouth.
Hannah could smell her warm pony smell.
Marmalade pawed at the ground.

"But you're real!" Hannah cried.

"I keep trying to tell you," Marmalade
said.

Hannah blinked several times to get the sleepiness out of her eyes. "I must be dreaming!"

"As you wish," said Marmalade. "Now, are you going to get on, or are we going to stand here all night? It's rather cold for someone as finely bred as myself."

"But how do I get on?" Hannah asked.

Marmalade seemed to think this was too silly a question to bother answering. She just turned her head round and pointed her nose at her back. Hannah saw that she was wearing a saddle, with shiny silver stirrups.

Hannah was still not quite sure. "Can I really . . .?"

Marmalade sneeze-snorted, and Hannah put her left foot in the stirrup and pulled herself up into the saddle.

"A little less of a thump next time, please," Marmalade said, pawing the ground again. "Now, if you'll just put your feet in the stirrups and hold on to the reins —"

"Don't move. I'll fall off," Hannah said in alarm, doing as she was told.

"Of course you won't. We're moving already, hadn't you noticed?"

Hannah stared around her. She thought they had been in her bedroom just a few moments ago, by the wardrobe-stable, but now they were out in the street and the houses were flashing by on each side, making her remember taking off in an aeroplane when they'd gone on a holiday

to Spain. It was just like that now; and
even more like it when Hannah saw the
ground a long way underneath them, with
the street lamps strung out like beads, and
the sky above like a big black tent studded
with tiny lights. Hannah gave a shriek of

terror which came out as a shriek of
delight. Her feet were firmly in the
stirrups and her hands gripped the green
leather reins and Marmalade's thick
mane, and she felt quite safe. She was
really riding, and not just riding, but flying!

Marmalade seemed to be in a better mood now that they were airborne.

"Isn't this better than staying in bed?" she called to Hannah.

"Oh, yes!" Hannah gasped as they cleared the dual carriageway. It was like a cross-country course in the sky! Marmalade plunged and dashed and circled and dived. She soared past the steelworks, skimmed over the school, swooped over

the swimming-pool, hovered over the hospital, leaped over the library, plummeted over the playing-fields, banked over the building site, and floated over the factories with a flick of her tail. Then she slowed down, falling like a feather towards a row of chimneys which Hannah recognized as her own road.

Hannah's insides felt dizzy and shaken, and she closed her eyes and held tight.

When she opened her eyes again, she was in bed, clutching her pillow. She felt as if she had been asleep for a very long time.

"I must have dreamed it all," she thought. She sat up and looked at the wardrobe-stable. Marmalade was there, propped up on her pole. Her button eyes seemed to be looking at Hannah and her painted mouth was curved in the beginning of a smile.

At breakfast, Hannah yawned. Mum said, "What's the matter with you, dozy-head? Aren't you awake yet?"

"I had a tiring night," Hannah said, wondering whether anyone would believe her. "I've been riding Marmalade all night long."

Mum smiled and ruffled Hannah's hair. "You always did have a good imagi-nation," she said.

All day at school, Hannah wondered whether it really was just her imagination. Would Marmalade turn into a real pony *every* night?

Perhaps, if I think about midnight-riding when I go to bed, she thought, it might happen again. But then will it be real, or just a dream?

She thought hard about Marmalade when she got into bed, but she was dreaming about teddy bears and liquorice allsorts when Marmalade clopped over to the bed and nudged her awake.

"Come on," Marmalade said, shaking her mane. "What are you sleeping for? I need exercise. I had to stand in this wardrobe for seven or eight hours while you were at school."

Hannah sat up and rubbed her eyes. "You *are* real!"

"Hrrrrmmph!" Marmalade said in disgust. "How much proof can a person want?"

"I'm sorry," Hannah said. "I —"

"Consider it from my point of view," Marmalade said. "You wouldn't be very pleased if I kept telling *you* you're not real, would you? Now hurry up and get on. I feel energetic. I'll show you I'm real all right."

Hannah put on her dressing-gown, took hold of the green reins and climbed up to the saddle, remembering not to crash down this time.

"Ready," she called.

"I hope you are," Marmalade said, with a quick hop on all four feet, like a lamb. "You'd better hold tight. I feel alphabetical tonight. I'm going to arabesque and bascule —"

"What do those words mean?" asked Hannah.

"Hold on and I'll show you," said Marmalade, and she was already in the air, aimed like an arrow, bounding over the railway bridge.

"I'm going to cavort and canter and caper," shouted Marmalade. "I feel like dancing and darting and dodging. I'm going to execute an effortless foxtrot and fandango, I'm going to frisk and flutter, gyrate and gallivant . . ." And she did.

"Gambol and gallop," shouted Hannah, getting the idea. "Hop, hurdle and hoof it –"

"Very funny," said Marmalade, "if we must indulge in inane idiocy. Hold on, I'm going to jig and jive, kick and kink, leap and lurch and – now hold really tight –"

"I am," cried Hannah.

"*Loop the loop!*"

And she did, an enormous sky-circle, so that the wind rushed through Hannah's hair and the stars were all around her, and she didn't know which way was up.

"That was rather good, if I say so myself," Marmalade said, levelling out over the sports centre. "I feel rather proud. I've never tried that before. Not feeling seasick, I hope?"

"Just a bit," Hannah said, not wanting to stop the aerobatics.

"All right, I'll slow down," Marmalade said. "I'll amble and brake and crawl and dawdle . . ."

But before she could get very far into the alphabet, Hannah was asleep.

Chapter 4

Next morning, Hannah remembered what Marmalade had said about being shut in the wardrobe all day. She carried her downstairs and out into the garden, and propped her up against the garden fence. While she was doing this, she couldn't help seeing that Marmalade was just a toy, made out of painted wood. Marmalade was stiff and lifeless in her hands, and her almost-smile was just a painted line on the wooden head.

The man-next-door's granddaughter was in her garden, wandering about as if she had nothing much to do. When she saw Hannah she said, "Hello," rather shyly, and Hannah said, "Hello," back, and they both looked at each other. Then the other girl ran back indoors. She had a long black glossy plait which bounced on her back as she ran, and she wore silky trousers and a tunic in colours as bright as jewels.

"Her name's Mariam," Dad said, when

Hannah told him that she had spoken to the girl next door. "She spends every Saturday here with her granddad. Her parents run a stall at the market." He had had plenty of time to chat to Mariam's granddad over the garden fence.

"Why don't you ask if she'd like to come in and play with you?" Mum said. "You could show her Marmalade."

Hannah was doubtful. She wasn't sure that Mariam would want to – to say nothing of Marmalade. "I don't know," she said. "Marmalade's a bit tired today. She did a lot of galloping about last night."

She saw Mum and Dad smile at each other. They thought it was just a game she had made up. Hannah looked out of the window at Marmalade and saw a toy hobby-horse sagging against the fence, and wondered for a moment whether they were right.

That night, she went to sleep thinking about Marmalade as usual. Some while later she opened her eyes and saw that Marmalade was still in her wardrobe-stable. The pony looked sad. Her head hung low and her ears drooped.

"What's the matter?" Hannah asked, getting out of bed. "Aren't you coming out?"

"I don't feel in the mood," Marmalade said grumpily.

"But it's the middle of the night," Hannah said, "and we've still got half the alphabet to do!"

"I know," said Marmalade.

"Don't you want to go out at all? Not for a –" Hannah had been practising all day – "a scamper or a skitter, a sidle or a scuttle, not even a single shuffling sidestep?"

"No," said Marmalade sadly. "I feel more like sulking in my stable."

"What's the matter?" Hannah asked. "Are you ill? Shall I fetch a – a vet, or ask Dad to give you a new coat of varnish?"

"No," Marmalade said. "I'm not ill."

"Then what *is* wrong?"

Marmalade looked at Hannah. "I'm lonely. I want a friend."

"Oh, I see," Hannah said.

"Another pony, I mean," Marmalade said. "You're not too bad, but there are some things only another pony can understand."

"Hmm," said Hannah. She stood for a moment thinking. Then she had an idea. "I'll see what I can do tomorrow," she said.

"Thank you. And now, if you don't mind, I'd like to get some sleep," Marmalade said, yawning.

Next day, Hannah took Marmalade out to the garden fence again, and propped her up so that she faced into Mariam's granddad's garden. Two or three times during the day she saw the old man looking at Marmalade, and later she saw him talking to Dad over the fence.

"I think my idea might be working," she told Marmalade that night.

"You're going to find me a friend?" Marmalade said, cheering up.

"Well . . . I hope so."

"This calls for a celebration," Marmalade neighed, undoing the door-bolt with her teeth and trotting out of the wardrobe. "Jump on!"

"Where are we going?" Hannah asked, scrambling up.

"Surprise!" Marmalade shouted. As soon as they were airborne, she set off in a straight line, instead of wheeling and circling as she had done before. Holding tightly, Hannah looked down and saw the silver threads of motorways, the dark huddled woods, clusters of sparkly lights for towns and villages, and once an inky black lake. Ahead, the moon hung in the sky like a big shiny coin.

"Are we going to the moon?" Hannah asked.

Marmalade snorted. "Of course not. I can't fly that far. Wait and see."

Not far ahead, the land was coming to an end. Hannah could smell the saltiness of the sea; below were the sharp cutaway shapes of white cliffs. Waves creamed at the sea's edge, and the moonlight cast a shining rippled track on the sea, leading to the distant place where sea and sky met.

We must have flown for miles and miles, Hannah thought. She shouted to Marmalade, "Are we going to France?"

"*Non!* But hold very tight – we're going down!"

Hannah gripped two handfuls of Marmalade's thick mane and got ready. She thought Marmalade was going to fly down

and land on the beach. Instead, she
headed straight on, out to sea, along the
moon's shimmering path. They were so
low over the waves that salty droplets got
into Hannah's mouth and clung to her
hair. She thought she could see the

darting shapes of fish beneath the water, blue and grey glints, flashing back the moonlight. Close by, a dark wave humped itself and then broke free to leap into the air, a glossy arching shape in a shower of moon-drops. A dolphin! Its mouth seemed to be laughing at them and it joined in their mad gallop out to sea, keeping pace with Marmalade, leaping and diving like a switchback ride, while the fish beneath the surface shimmered like silver fireworks. And then Marmalade was slowing, her hooves sending plumes of spray up from the waves. The dolphin stood up on its tail and back-paddled, and chattered goodbye. Then it dived and was gone.

We've come a very long way, Hannah thought, miles and miles, far too far to get back again in one night . . .

But before she had finished thinking, she was waking up from a long sleep, yawning and stretching. She looked across at Marmalade, who was smiling her secret smile again.

"That was a very good celebration," Hannah said. She thought to herself, I hope there really *is* something to celebrate.

When she went downstairs, she let herself out into the garden and tiptoed towards the shed. The door was firmly shut, but she could hear Dad inside, whistling. Through the cobwebby window she could see strips of red leather hanging on a peg. She smiled and crept away.

Chapter 5

That Saturday morning, Hannah saw Dad out in the garden quite early, talking to Mariam's granddad over the fence. Dad came indoors looking very pleased with himself. While he ate his breakfast, he kept looking at his watch. Then he said, "Come outside with me, Hannah. It's time for Mariam's surprise."

"What surprise?" Hannah said, although she had guessed.

"It's her birthday today," Dad said, "and her granddad asked me to make a special present for her."

There was a ring at the doorbell.

"That will be them now," Mum said.

She went to open the front door. Mariam came through to the kitchen, holding her granddad's hand. She looked rather shy because of being in someone else's house, but she smiled at Hannah.

She had brown eyes as lively as a robin's and she wore silky trousers and a tunic of bright turquoise, like a kingfisher. It was decorated with gold and scarlet braid, and she had gold and scarlet ribbons plaited into her hair, to match. Everyone else's clothes suddenly looked very dull.

"Happy birthday," everyone said to Mariam.

Dad led the way out to the garden and then he made Mariam wait with her eyes closed just as he had made Hannah wait. He went into the shed and brought out Mariam's hobby-horse – a pony like Marmalade, a little darker in colour. It had a mane and forelock of pure white wool; it had pricked felt ears, and a bridle made of red leather. Its mouth was curved into the beginning of a smile.

Mariam clapped her hands and laughed, and hugged the pony.

"He is a magician, your father," Mariam's granddad said to Hannah.

"I know," Hannah said. She wondered whether Dad knew how *much* of a magician he was. "I must fetch Marmalade," she said.

"What will Mariam's pony be called?" Mum said. "Is it a he or a she?"

Mariam looked at her pony and then at
Hannah. "Yours is called Marmalade, isn't
she?" she said. "I think mine is called
Mango Chutney. I shall call him Chutney
for short."

"That's a funny name for a pony," said
Mariam's granddad.

"Chutney likes it," said Mariam,
cuddling the horse. "Don't you,
Chutney?"

Hannah went upstairs to fetch Marmalade. Something was worrying her. She told Marmalade about the new pony. "Will Chutney be a magic pony, like you are?" she asked.

"That depends on Mariam," Marmalade said. "It depends whether she thinks he's a few bits of wood and leather, or whether she thinks he's a pony."

Hannah sighed with relief. "Then it will be all right," she said.

Chapter 6

"You must decide what to wear for the birthday party," Mum said to Hannah when Mariam and her granddad had gone back next door. "It was nice of Mariam to invite you, wasn't it?"

"Mmmm," Dad said. He was busy making a list.

"What are you planning now?" Hannah said.

"Well," Dad said, looking more pleased than ever, "while you were upstairs, Mariam's granddad asked me to make lots more ponies. Mariam's mum and dad run a toy stall at the market. They like to sell handmade things. So I'm going to make

them some. And perhaps –" Dad said, getting carried away, "– perhaps, if they do well, I might think about having a stall f my own! It'd be better than hanging ound the Job Centre."

"You and your ideas," Mum said. "Pigs might fly. Still, it's worth a try."

Hannah opened her mouth to say, "Ponies can fly, so why shouldn't pigs?" but then realized how silly it would sound. She caught Dad's eye and he grinned, and then he wrote down something else on his list. She looked over his shoulder. He had written: Pink paint, corkscrews for tails.

Hannah smiled, thinking of a skyful of flying pigs, zooming around like fat pink balloons when you blow them up and then let go without tying up the end.

"Come on," Mum said. "You still haven't decided what to wear. I'll need to iron something."

"Oh yes," Hannah said, thinking of the party. It was a long time since she'd been to a party. Mariam had invited her so that they could ride their ponies together, and groom them, and talk about them. Mariam wanted to be friends. Her plan had worked better than she had expected; they could all be friends now.

Mariam and Hannah.

Marmalade and Chutney.